KEITH BRUMPTON

SUPERHEROES DOWN THE PLUGHOLE

Splendid stuff!

MACDONALD YOUNG BOOKS

PROLOGUE

A brief history of Britain's superheroes...

A man called Harry Blanchard is widely credited as being Britain's first superhero. A former circus strongman, Blanchard became a national hero in 1887, when he single handedly prevented the steamship SS Scarborough from sinking. Overnight he became a hero, and the idea of the superhero was born...

ALFORD ACADEMY

This book is to be returned on or before the last date stamped below.

Brumpton, Keith

Superheroes
down the
plughole

1501727

For J. T. Robinson

Text and illustrations copyright © Keith Brumpton 1999

First published in Great Britain in 1999
by Macdonald Young Books
an imprint of Wayland Publishers Ltd
61 Western Road
Hove
East Sussex
BN3 1JD

The right of Keith Brumpton to be identified as the author
and illustrator of this Work has been asserted by him in
accordance with the Copyright, Designs and Patents Act 1988.

Typeset by McBride Design
Printed in Hong Kong

British Library Cataloguing in Publication Data available

ISBN 0 7500 2857 2

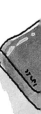

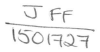

Sensing a need, Harry Blanchard employed other superheroes. Ex-trapeze artists, boxers, and Henry Gilligan, the first superhero to wear a cloak with his name on it. Gilligan was a butcher from Croydon and earned his spurs saving an airship over Bombay on 12 June 1911.

"Wee" Harry Gilligan, the Flying Anvil

Tilda Snetterton, the world's first female superhero

The years from 1900-1950 were the golden age of British superheroes. Then, in the fifties, American heroes began to cross the Atlantic. They were fitter and stronger than their British counterparts, and the public turned to them in great numbers.

Raymond Bond ← 'The Red Kestrel', August 1951

By the end of the millenium, Britain had only twelve superheroes in active service. The glory days of Harry Blanchard seemed far off indeed.

Old Stretchy's Back

Elasticman's alarm clock began to ring. It span round and round on the shelf above his bed, before landing with a crash on top of the sleeping superhero's head.

He sat up with a sudden jerk, which didn't really help his arthritis. It was seven-thirty in the morning, and Elasticman felt about a hundred years old. The day had dawned chill, and a draughty breeze was blowing up his Lycra leggings. He could hear the sound of his friend, Skeletonman, snoring in the bunk below.

Normally the day would have begun with a bowl of cold porridge in the dining room, but three days ago, Matron had called him to her office. He could still remember her exact words.

Matron's cat

"This old place is falling apart and we don't have the funds to repair it. I'm going to have to find a new home where I can look after you lot. A home for distressed sailors has just come on to the market, but it's down south, so I'm leaving you in charge while I go and take a look. You're the oldest and the only one that's half sensible."

Elasticman smiled, proudly.

"But I warn you, any trouble and you'll get no pocket money for six months. If anything goes wrong I'll hold you responsible. OK?"

"I…"

"Good. I've left £10 housekeeping money on top of the fridge. Lights out at 8p.m. I'll be back by the end of the week."

And with that she'd gone, leaving Elasticman in charge of the home, a group of superheroes who'd lost their powers, and a three-legged cat called Greg. It was a big responsibility!

Elasticman was shuffling through the hallway on his way to pick up the mail when he passed one of the new residents, Hamsterman.

"Morning, Hammy."

"Morning, Elastic. See you for *Neighbours* later."

Elasticman bent down to pick up the mail. And that's when he saw the letter for the first time.

There are all sorts of nasty letters you can get through the post. Big bills. Letters telling you that one of your library books was due back in 1964, or that your pet alligator has been bothering the neighbours again.

Elasticman didn't think, at first, that this would be one of those. It had a nice stamp and, from what he could tell without his reading glasses, seemed to have been posted from America. He opened the large white envelope and began to read.

His face immediately took on a gloomy air. His shoulders drooped as though he'd been playing in goal for Hartlepool United.

Dept. Superhero Inspectorate
Superhero Inspectorate
10th Avenue
New York
USA tel: 00 44566 657657/8

Dear Matron Mandible

This is to remind you that

The Mandible Rest Home for Superheroes,
196 Chimney Hill, UK

is now due for its three-yearly inspection.
Our inspectors will accordingly call on

Friday 13 November

in order to:

1. Tour the facilities and meet your superheroes.
2. Carry out tests.
3. Issue a certificate of success according to the results obtained, or if necessary, withdraw certification.

Our Inspector will call at **10am.**

Yours sincerely

ATOM GIRL

Elasticman read the letter again, but it seemed just as bad second time round.

The home was going to be inspected by some hotshot heroes from the USA. If it failed, the home would be closed.

His thin, wobbly legs needed a seat.

"What can I do?" he wondered. "Who can a failed superhero turn to in his hour of need?"

A Summit or Summat

Laura Putney looked out of the bus window as it passed the football field where Fowlmouth Pensioners were playing the team from Her Majesty's Prison, Welworne-under-Ware.

It then climbed Chimney Hill, overtaking an overweight golden retriever en route, before pulling in at a familiar stop by the golf course.

Laura ran all the way to the Mandible Rest Home. She'd had a call that morning from a depressed-sounding Elasticman, asking if they could meet up because he urgently needed some advice.

But what about Matron? Aren't visitors forbidden?

Elasticman took a deep breath and explained the whole story: about Matron being away, and about the inspection, and about what would happen if the home was shut down and they lost their right to remain superheroes. And then, just to show the sort of day he was having, his biscuit fell apart while he was dunking it in his tea.

Laura took his hand.

"Don't worry, Elastic. We'll sort something out. Things are never as bad as they look."

Elasticman's eyes seemed to brighten behind his mask.

"Do you really think we can pass the inspection and keep the home going until Matron gets back?"

"Of course we can. You *are* superheroes aren't you?"

(In the distance she could hear the sound of Mothgirl as she crashed into a garden shed during take-off. This was going to be tough!)

Miss Motivator

One-two, one-two, one-two!

Limbs creaked, costumes split, superheroes groaned. Laura's get-fit programme had begun and there were a lot of grumbles.

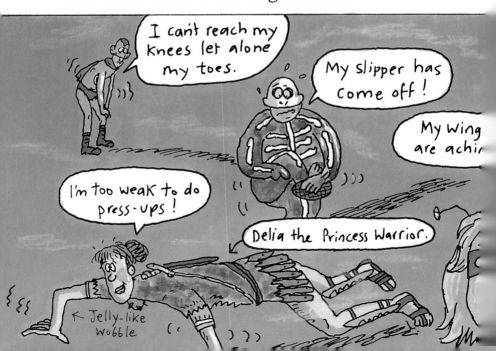

I can't reach my knees let alone my toes.

My slipper has come off!

My wing are achir

I'm too weak to do press-ups!

Delia the Princess Warrior.

Jelly-like wobble

"There's an inspection in two days' time and unless we all try our best, the home will be shut down!" Laura said firmly. "Look," she said, "you can have a break after the training run."

"How far is the run?" asked Hamsterman, in a nervous, squeaky voice.

"Just round the grounds."

"Round the grounds!" gasped Skeletonman. "That's miles! I'll never make it."

Laura had to admit that Skeletonman's face did look a funny colour as he ran. A sort of pinky-purple. And she felt sorry for Delia the Princess Warrior when her ankle twisted as she trod on an old Polo mint.

But even so, she was still shocked at how out of shape the superheroes really were.

Elasticman sank down on to a park bench and sucked on his inhaler.

"I'm sorry, Laura. The old knee has given way again. It got damaged during an incident at the Empire State Building in 1942. Never been the same since."

"Don't worry," said Laura, "at least you gave it your best shot. I'm a bit worried about the others though. Don't they want our get-fit plan to work?"

"Of course they do," wheezed the elderly hero, his jumpsuit covered in perspiration. "They just need a little more time."

"Time is one thing we don't have," sighed Laura.

Friday the Thirteenth – Part One

Laura stepped back and admired her handiwork.

The new sign over the main entrance looked, she thought, very professional.

Elasticman had been busy fixing loose floorboards in the lounge. The carpet between the sofa and the TV had become very worn since someone lost the remote control, so he'd put a rug over the barest patches.

Just as they were enjoying a well-earned cup of tea, there came a knock at the lounge door. It was Skeletonman and Mothgirl.

Mothgirl's antennae had drooped out of sight, usually a sign that she was unhappy. Skeletonman pushed her forward.

"Mothgirl has something to tell you."

We're sorry, Laura, but we don't want to take the superhero test. We're not ready for it. We'd only flunk.

Yeah. Thanks for trying and everything, but Matron was right, we're just no good.

Sorry...

Elasticman looked silently down at his old boots.

Mothgirl turned on her way out.

"If we pack up and go, perhaps they'll leave the home open for real superheroes…"

Laura was left on her own, except for Greg the three-legged cat, who came and sat on her lap. The visitor from America was due in ten minutes.

Friday the Thirteenth – Part Two

It was a strong, loud ring. Laura opened the front door and there stood a tall, muscular figure with white teeth and a firm (very firm) handshake.

"Laura Putney… I, er, help out here. We've been expecting you. Come in."

"Thank you. Nice sign."

Laura asked Captain Justice if he'd had a good flight.

"Sure. I always say a superhero should fly the Atlantic every few weeks if only to keep the arms in good shape."

Laura took a deep breath.

"I'm sorry, Captain Justice, but the inspection will have to be called off. The superheroes are… er… they're um… they're not feeling well."

"Not feeling well? That's ridiculous! A real superhero doesn't get sick. He can't afford to."

Laura looked flustered.

The superheroes suddenly rose up from behind the reception desk. Elasticman patted Laura's back.

"It's all right, Laura, the... er... flu bug is over. We're... er... ready for action."

Captain Justice eyed the unusual group of individuals huddled before him.

"Never judge a book by its cover," mumbled Hamsterman.

"OK. Listen up, you guys. The Inspection will be in two parts. Firstly I'll inspect the building and its facilities."

"Secondly, you will have to prove your abilities as superheroes by solving the Titanium Grade Challenge which I have in this envelope."

Captain Justice opened the envelope slowly, prolonging the suspense a little.

Looking for Streptopongus

They'll never do it.

Captain Justice read from a piece of silvery card.

"Your task, superheroes, should you choose to accept it, is to... find a deadly virus hidden somewhere in your own building!" An excited murmur ran round the group. Captain Justice continued.

"Before my official arrival I infiltrated your building and have hidden a deadly, flesh-eating virus called Streptopongus B. To pass the test, you must locate the virus and place it in this sealed container. You have one hour, starting from... now!"

Captain Justice blew a whistle to signal the start of the test.

The superheroes began to fly round in different directions, eagerly searching for the virus. There were one or two mid-air collisions before Elasticman suggested they settle down and organize themselves. Mothgirl was the best at flying, so she would check the roof. Skeletonman could squeeze through cracks in the floorboards, so he'd look there, and so on, until everyone had a job to do.

Laura felt quite proud. Was there a chance her clapped-out band of superheroes could actually pull this one off?

firmly crossed

Skeletonman was trapped between two floorboards in the attic. How he now regretted those three extra chocolate eclairs he'd had for breakfast! Mothgirl, meanwhile, had flown into the bathroom light and damaged a wing. Delia the Princess Warrior was temporarily out of action after slipping on a pair of rollerskates in the girls' dormitory.

33

In the kitchen, Hamsterman was making himself a poached egg. It wasn't that he'd given up the search for the deadly virus, he just needed a snack to keep himself going.

"There we go… one poached egg… add a little pepper and, hey presto! Huh?"

Hamsterman was surprised to find not one poached egg, but two. One of the poached eggs was pulsing and seemed to be getting larger…

"Rotating rodents!" he sqeaked. "This ain't no poached egg, this is the virus!"

Hamsterman scuttled to the kitchen door and shouted for help.

Mothgirl was first to hear his call. She straightened her damaged wing and fluttered downstairs as fast as she could.

She was joined by Skeletonman (who had a couple of painful splinters in his bottom), and Delia the Princess Warrior. Elasticman and Laura arrived seconds later.

"Look at the way it's attacking the kitchen bench."

It was true. The deadly Streptopongus B virus was spreading, like a grotesque pizza, eating everything in its path.

"Get the container Captain Justice gave to us!" wheezed Elasticman, still breathless from running.

Skeletonman passed the container to Elasticman who dropped it.

The virus was making gurgling noises and moving down the kitchen bench. It had eaten Hamsterman's egg and the plate. Now it was moving in on the pint-sized superhero himself.

"My sandwich box!" cried Mothgirl.
"That'll do as a container. It seals in flavour,
so it should work with viruses too."

"Good thinking!" beamed Elasticman. He
grabbed hold of a ladle and flicked the
Streptopongus into the air
like some toxic pancake.

Delia the Princess Warrior grabbed the sandwich box from Mothgirl and skated forward as fast as she could, catching the virus just centimetres from the floor.

Before you could say "bacterial infection" she had the lid on the lunch box and it was safely in the fridge.

Laura and the superheroes gave her a little round of applause. Laura's eyes were brimming with tears of pride (or was that just from Skeletonman's onion sandwich?).

Somehow, against all odds, her raggle-taggle crew of superheroes had found the deadly Streptopongus and made it safe. She couldn't wait to see Captain Justice's face.

feeling a bit faint →

Very hungry ↓

← Dazed but happy

Captain Justice sigh!!

relieved smile ↓

Enter the Squirrel...

Captain Justice shook Elasticman by the hand.

"Well done, Plasticman."

"Er, it's Elasticman."

The superheroes seemed to grow an extra metre in stature.

"Hamsterman was right. You should never judge a book by its cover. I haven't completed my report yet, but I can tell you guys, off the record, that you passed the test with flying colours. It was a mighty impressive display."

"I'll be getting back to the States now. I want to hand this virus over to our top government scientists – they'll make it safe. I'll return your sandwich box as soon as we've scraped off the poisonous gunge."

Mothgirl fluttered her eyelashes at Captain Justice.

The American took off from the driveway, and soared like an arrow up into the darkening skies. It wasn't long before he reached cruising altitude over the town. Letting the lunch box fall from his hands, he allowed himself a chuckle. There had been no deadly virus – he'd used a poached egg instead of actual Streptopongus. It would have been foolish to use anything dangerous when in the company of such a clapped-out bunch of superheroes.

How on earth had they passed the test? Oh well, it wasn't his problem, they'd probably never have to deal with any real emergencies in a little town like that anyway.

Mothgirl's lunch box continued to fall and landed in a ditch just outside Fewercome Bay. There, the old poached egg began to react with some pesticides and a piece of stale cheese. A week later the contents were eaten by a foraging squirrel.

Laura was at home watching *Neighbours* and could hardly believe her eyes.

This sounded like a job for Elasticman and his superheroes. Now where had she put that telephone number…?

Retired superhero, power-crazed villain, or disillusioned squirrel trainer, there's a Keith Brumpton book for you!

Superheroes Gone Bust

The superheroes in Fowlmouth-under-Lime have a few problems. Elasticman goes slack under pressure. Mothgirl can't avoid bright lights. And Skeletonman is very overweight for a skeleton. But Laura is convinced that all they need is a crime to solve. Enter the Skunk...

Tanya, the Moo-vie

It's hard work being a superhero, so Tanya, Hoofed Crusader decides to take a well-earned holiday touring Moo York, Mexi-cow and Mos-cow. Then she receives an emergency call. Owlhoot Farm has been taken over by UFOs (Unidentified Furry Objects)! It's time for Tanya, Hoofed Crusader to take to the skies...

Look Out, Loch Ness Monster

For as long as he could remember, Kevin McAllister has had one ambition – to be the first person to see the Loch Ness Monster. Every night he watches the loch through his telescope, hoping that Nessie will appear. Then one moonlit night, Kevin sees a huge shadow moving across the water like a torpedo with bumps...

You can buy all these books from your local bookseller, or they can be ordered direct from the publisher. For more information, write to: *The Sales Department, Macdonald Young Books, 61 Western Road, Hove, East Sussex BN3 1JD*